W9-DJI-192

Can you catch Josephine?

Stéphane Poulin

Tundra Books

My name is Daniel and I live with my father in Montreal.
My cat's name is Josephine.
Sometimes she gives me a lot of trouble.

Every morning before I go to school,
  I hug my father and say goodbye to Josephine.
Yesterday, I could not find her.

In the schoolyard I met my friend Christiane.
"What's in your schoolbag?" she asked.
It was Josephine.

It was too late to take her home.
What could I do?

I hid her in my desk.
But she stuck her paw out and made the kids laugh.

Mr. Martin turned around.
"What's going on here?" he shouted. "OPEN THAT DESK."

He should not have asked me to do that.

Josephine jumped out.

Mr. Martin shouted: "CATCH THAT CAT."
The kids laughed and tried to grab her.

But she was too fast.
She jumped from desk to desk, and then up to the window.

She was going to jump into the schoolyard.
When she saw the janitor, she changed her mind.

She ran up the tree to the third floor.
I saw her go into the library.

Mr. Martin yelled at the class: "Get back to your seats."
Mr. Martin yelled at me: "Catch that cat."

I ran up to the library.
Mrs. Denis looked up from her book.

"Why the big hurry?" she asked. "What are you looking for?"
"Josephine," I said.
"Look under the letter 'J', " she said.
She thought Josephine was a book!

"Josephine is a CAT," I said.
"Then look under the letter 'C', " she said.

Josephine must be very smart.
She was hiding on the 'J' shelf.
As soon as I saw her, she jumped down and ran off again.

What a chase! Down the stairs, around the second floor, back down the stairs, around the first floor, she ran.

The bell rang. Kids came into the halls, but they were too surprised to help. Then Josephine gave me real trouble.

She went where I cannot go – into the girls' washroom.

I ran and got Christiane.
"Help me catch Josephine," I said.

Christiane went into the washroom and came back out.
"She's not there," she said.

Then Josephine ran out the door right through our legs.

They should keep the door to the science room closed.

When there is no class there, the blinds are down.
It's the scariest room in the school.

I looked in fast.
Eyes stared at me.
I could not see Josephine.

I went out into the hall to wait.

Soon Josephine ran out.

This time she went down to the gym.

"My cat," I yelled. "Help me catch her."
Mr. Atlas shouted to the class: "Everybody! After it!"

We all ran after Josephine.
She went back up the stairs.

At last she ran into trouble.

Mrs. Bruno was coming down the stairs with her class.
The gym class was running up the stairs with me.

Josephine was caught between us.

"TAKE THAT CAT TO THE PRINCIPAL'S OFFICE," Mrs. Bruno shou

I held Josephine very tight all the way.
"Don't be scared," I told her, as I knocked on the office door.

When I opened it, I got a big surprise.

The principal had a cat on her desk.

"Who's that with you?" she asked.
"Josephine," I said. "She came to school this morning."

"This is Tiger," she said.
"He came to school this morning, too.
Dear me, you and I have the same trouble.
What shall we do?

"I know.
If Josephine comes to school again, bring her to my office.
She can wait for you here.
But don't tell anyone."

And I didn't tell anyone.
But Josephine must have told.

Because this morning four cats came to school.

To Lise and Gabriel, the colors of your smiles

© 1987, Stéphane Poulin

ISBN 0-88776-198-4 hardcover 10, 9, 8, 7, 6, 5, 4, 3, 2
ISBN 0-88776-214-X paperback 10, 9, 8, 7, 6, 5, 4, 3, 2

Published in Canada by Tundra Books, Montreal, Quebec H3G 1R4

Published in the United States by Tundra Books of Northern New York, Plattsburgh, NY 12901

Library of Congress Catalog Card Number 87-50374

Canadian Cataloguing in Publication Data: Poulin, Stéphane. Can you catch Josephine? Issued also in French under the title: Peux-tu attraper Joséphine? ISBN 0-88776-198-4. I. Title. II. Title: Peux-tu attraper Joséphine? PS8581.0846P4913 1987 jC843'.54 C87-090107-9 PZ10.3.P69Ca 1987

The publisher has applied funds from its Canada Council block grant for 1987 toward the editing and production of this book.

Color transparencies and separations: TechnoCouleur Inc., Montreal

The paintings from this book have been given a solo exhibition at the Shayne Gallery, Montreal.

Foreign Edition: Swedish, 1988, Carlsen if, Stockholm, Sweden

Printed in Belgium

4224